First published in North America
by Annick Press, 2006
Text © 2006 Meg Clibbon
Illustrations © 2006 Lucy Clibbon
Originally published by Zero to Ten Limited
(a member of the Evans Publishing Group)
© 2006 Zero to Ten Limited

Cataloging in Publication
Clibbon, Meg
Magical Creatures / Man Eating Meg, Loch Ness Lucy.

ISBN-13: 978-1-55451-030-6 (bound)
ISBN-10: 1-55451-030-9 (bound)
ISBN-13: 978-1-55451-029-0 (pbk.)
ISBN-10: 1-55451-029-5 (pbk.)

1. Animals, Mythical--Juvenile literature. 2. Monsters--Juvenile
literature. I. Clibbon, Lucy II. Title.

GR825.C486 2006   j398.24'54   C2006-901257-1

www.annickpress.com

Printed in China

MAGICAL CREATURES

Man-eating Meg

Man-eating Meg used to like eating
people, but now she prefers fresh fruit,
salad, and smoked salmon. Fortunately
she was *never* tempted to eat children –
otherwise they would never read her books!

Loch Ness Lucy

Loch Ness Lucy is half artist,
half human, and lives far far away in
an imaginary world. Little is known
about this rare and mysterious
creature as few have seen her.

For Magical Mary with Love x

Annick Press Ltd.

Magical Creatures

The world is full of interesting things that we can touch and smell and hear. Our eyes can see the wonders of nature and the busy world all around us. But our imagination enables us to step into another world full of mystery and magic. Wonderful creatures live there who have the power to fascinate, frighten, or enchant us. Some have been part of folklore for generations. Some creatures live in a half-world where no one is quite sure if they exist or not. This book is a collection of some of Meg and Lucy's favorite and most magical creatures.

Dragons

There is nothing soft about a dragon. Scales as hard as flint cover its flesh and muscles and bones. The cracks between its scales are filled with metal and stones, but the metal is gold and the stones are rubies, diamonds, and amethysts from the dragon's nest of treasure. The dragon sleeps on its nest with its long strong tail curled around its body.

No birds dare sing near the dragon's lair and no soft little animals live nearby, for the dragon will seek them out with a sharp glittering eye. Front claws that can delicately turn and caress precious stones tear soft things to pieces with dagger-like cruelty. Huge leathery wings carry the dragon over many miles in search of prey. It breathes fire from its mouth, and smoke and steam billow from its nostrils.

And yet this most fearsome creature has one weak spot. There is always a chink somewhere in its armor, a tiny gap between its scales, and through this chink it is soft and vulnerable ... so all dragons can be defeated by those clever enough to find that one weak place and brave enough to try.

Unicorns

Imagine a beautiful horse with smooth, white glossy hair, a silver mane and tail, and silver shining hooves. Imagine a single horn, straight and pointed but wonderfully patterned, coming from that horse's forehead. Then imagine soft brown eyes full of wisdom and magical power looking deep into your eyes. Graceful as they usually are, unicorns often get their horns caught in the undergrowth.

Pegasus

A horse is a most beautiful animal. It has slender and graceful legs but a broad back, a powerful rump, and a noble arching neck. Pegasus had all the beauty of a horse, as well as a pair of strong wings to carry him soaring in the air with tail and mane flowing around him. This amazing horse comes from Greek mythology – he was born from the drops of blood that fell from the head of the Medusa when Perseus cut off her head (see "Gorgons").

Giants

There is no disguising the fact that giants are big. Whole valleys and hillsides tremble when a giant walks about on his huge feet. Little birds sitting in their treetop nests fly away in shock when a giant looks down at them. Lady giants wear such huge petticoats that fishermen could use them for sails on their fishing boats, and they could catch fish in the men's giant string undershirts.

Giants look like human beings and are similar in personality. However, there is one big difference: giants have very small brains. This doesn't matter a bit if a giant is good-tempered, kind, and affectionate, but a small brain and a bad-tempered personality go badly together. Such giants (and people) can be unpleasant and dangerous.

Dwarves

Dwarves are the opposite of giants. A dwarf has a small body and a big brain. Dwarves are quick and clever and can be cunning. They wear long woolly hats on their heads to keep their brains warm and ready for action. They like mining underground for gold and precious stones. Frequent battles break out between dwarves who work for this treasure and the dragons who steal it.

Ogres, Trolls, and Goblins

Ogres

Ogres are similar to giants – they are very big! However, there are several differences. Ogres are very, very ferocious, and they have disgusting habits. They are not very tidy and they leave half-eaten bones and potato chip bags all over their bedrooms. They never use a Kleenex. Oh yes – and they eat people.

Trolls

Trolls are like small ogres and they are bad-tempered, ugly, and fierce. They live in dark places such as caves or tree roots in deep forests. They are always hungry and they are not vegetarians.

Goblins

Goblins tend to think that everyone is picking on them. This is often true because goblins are miserable, dishonest, and sly with no sense of humor, so they are not very popular. Giants are always laughing at them and ogres like to eat them. Dwarves just ignore them.

Creatures of Watery Places

Kraken and Scolopendra

On no account go anywhere near these creatures. They live in the deepest oceans and they are huge. They are as strong as tree trunks and have mouths like caverns, and they love eating ships. They are not very lovable. The Kraken first appears in Norwegian stories from the 12th century, while the Scolopendra is Greek.

Mermaids

Mermaids live in crystal clear water far away from human beings, although they do like shipwrecks. Mermaids are very beautiful and sit on coral rocks, combing their hair and singing. Perhaps they cause some of the shipwrecks by distracting the poor sailors with their beautiful hair and heavenly singing.

The Loch Ness Monster

Many very clever people have searched for this creature in Loch (Lake) Ness, in Scotland, but it is too clever for them and so far it has kept its secrets.

The Bunyip

This bad-tempered little creature lives in Australia, where you would think it would be happy and friendly. However, it is not at all happy and friendly, and jumps out at people from the billabongs and other waterholes where it lives. It gives people such a fright that afterwards they cannot quite remember what it looked like.

The Sphinx

Gazing across the sands of the Egyptian desert is a huge statue of the Sphinx, reminding passersby of the monster of ancient Greece and Egypt. This monster had the body of a lion and the head of a smiling woman. It was very fearsome and, to make things worse, it asked anyone foolish enough to go near its cave this puzzling riddle:

What is it that goes on four legs in the morning, two at noon, and three in the evening?

The Sphinx threw anyone who failed to answer the riddle correctly over the precipice near its cave. Finally a young Greek warrior called Oedipus gave the Sphinx this answer:

Man crawls on all fours as a baby, then he walks on two legs, until in old age he needs a stick as a third leg.

He was right, and with a howl of rage the Sphinx threw itself over the precipice.

The Sphinx originally appears in ancient Egyptian mythology. The famous sphinx of Giza was built around 2600 BCE. The ancient Greeks thought he lived in the mountains of Ethiopia.

Gorgons

The Gorgons were three evil sisters who had wriggling seething snakes instead of hair. One of the three sisters was very beautiful. She was called Medusa and could turn anyone to stone just by looking into their eyes. Brave, handsome Perseus was very fond of beautiful women but not very fond of snakes. He defeated Medusa by looking at her through her reflection in a highly polished shield. Her evil gaze was powerless to hurt him and he killed her easily. Her sisters were roused to fury and chased after him, but Perseus escaped wearing a pair of magic winged sandals. Sadly, sandals like these are not generally available. In Greek mythology Medusa was born beautiful but made ugly by the goddess Athena. The winged horse Pegasus was born from drops of her blood mixed with sea foam.

The Phoenix

Golden sunbeams are the food of ancient Egypt's magical phoenix bird and dewdrops are its drink. It breathes life from the perfume of spices, sandalwood, cinnamon, and saffron. The phoenix never dies, but every 540 years it makes a special nest and here in the hot rays of the sun it is set alight. Flames lick around its beautiful iridescent body. Then, from the ashes of the nest, a new, even more beautiful bird arises, with purple plumage, blue and crimson tail, and golden ruff and crest. Note that a phoenix should never be kept in a wooden house. The ancient Greeks thought that the phoenix lived in Ethiopia, and renewed itself every 500 years.

Centaurs

Humans have always had a close relationship with horses, but never closer than in a centaur. A centaur is half man and half horse – the body of a horse and the upper body and head of a strong man. Centaurs carry a bow and arrow or spear on one shoulder and a musical instrument on the other. They love hunting and music, and they are very wise. The Greeks thought that centaurs lived in the lands to the north called Scythia.

Werewolves

When the night is dark but the moon is full, lock the doors and pull the curtains, for then the werewolves may be about. In the light of day they look like ordinary men. At sunset dark hairs start to grow on their hands and, as the moon rises and the dusk falls, a fearful change takes place. Soon their rough coats, pricked ears, lolling tongues, and gleaming fangs show that they have turned into wolves. With blood-curdling howls and quick glances of their blazing eyes, they bound away until dawn, when they return once again to human form.

The Yeti
(The Abominable Snowman)

Does the Yeti exist? It has made big footmarks in the snow and has been seen slipping like a dark shadow into the foothills of the great Himalayan mountains. The Yeti has been described as a large, hairy apelike creature by the nomadic tribesmen who live there. Perhaps we should believe them, or perhaps it is another creature who only lives in the imagination.

The Green Man

Deep in the heart of the British woods is a mysterious presence. Pearly sap rises in the trunks, and green leaves bend and twist as something strokes them. The essence and spirit of the woods can be glimpsed in the shape of a green shadowy man, twined about with living tendrils and blossoms, as he slips past and disappears into the forest glades.

The Griffin

A Griffin is a creature with the body of a lion and the wings and head of an eagle. The lion is the king of beasts – its kingdom is the Earth on which it walks with massive tawny paws. All the creatures of the Earth fear and respect the lion. The eagle is the king of the birds – its kingdom is the air in which it soars on massive golden wings. All the creatures who fly in the air look up to the eagle in awe.

The Griffin is massive and majestic in stature, far greater and more powerful then either the king of the Earth or the king of the air. The Griffin is brave and strong and hates injustice. Beware, those who do wrong – the Griffin may seek you out and punish you. The Griffin comes from ancient Egypt, and the Greeks believed their god Apollo rode one.

Salamanders

Salamanders are magical and poisonous lizards who live in fire and bask in flames. They come from glowing furnaces deep in the center of the Earth. When they crawl into the light, with their flickering tongues and burnished scales, their evil power can destroy anything in their path.

Fairies

Fairies, including pixies, sprites, elves, and gnomes, are small magical creatures who live in enchanted forests and woodlands. They have special powers to weave spells and spread their magic throughout the world to those who believe in them. There are many kinds of fairies, but nobody knows exactly what they look like. They are very secret, and once you have seen them, fairy dust blows into your eyes and you cannot quite remember anything about them – you just remember feeling happy.

You have now had a brief introduction to a few magical creatures, but there are lots more who can be found in stories from many lands. And perhaps there are some who live deep in your imagination, just waiting to come out and astonish us all!